A Classic Treasury of
Christmas

featuring the artwork of
Lynn Bywaters Ferris

Ideals Children's Books • Nashville, Tennessee

Published by Ideals Publishing Corporation
Nashville, Tennessee 37210

Printed and bound in the United States of America.

ISBN 0-8249-8524-9 (book)
ISBN 0-8249-7453-0 (set)

Library of Congress Cataloging-in-Publication Data

A classic treasury of Christmas/
[illustrations by Lynn Bywaters Ferris].
p.   cm.
Contents: The nativity—Away in a manger—Joy to the world
The night before Christmas—O Christmas tree—The fir tree
We wish you a merry Christmas—We three kings
The nutcracker—Up on the housetop—The first noel
Silent night—Yes, Virginia, there is a Santa Claus
The twelve days of Christmas.
ISBN 0-8249-8524-9 (book)
1. Christmas stories.   2. Carols, English—Texts.
I. Ferris, Lynn Bywaters.
PN6071.C6C67   1991
808.8'033—dc20   91-19276
CIP

The illustrations in this book were rendered in
guache on watercolor paper.
The text type was set in Goudy.
The display type was set in Caslon.
Color separations were made by Web Tech,
Butler, Wisconsin.
Printed and bound by Arcata Graphics Kingsport,
Kingsport, Tennessee.

Designed by Stacy Venturi-Pickett.

Table of Contents

The Nativity

The Gospel According to St. Luke and St. Matthew
from *The King James Bible*

And it came to pass in those days, that there went out a decree from Cæsar Augustus, that all the world should be taxed. And all went to be taxed, every one into his own city. And Joseph also went up from Galilee, out of the city of Nazareth, into Judæa, unto the city of David, which is called Bethlehem; (because he was of the house and lineage of David:) to be taxed with Mary his espoused wife, being great with child.

And so it was, that, while they were there, the days were accomplished that she should be delivered. And she brought forth her firstborn son, and wrapped him in swaddling clothes, and laid him in a manger; because there was no room for them in the inn.

And there were in the same country shepherds abiding in the field, keeping watch over their flock by night. And, lo, the angel of the Lord came upon them, and the glory of the Lord shone round about them: and they were sore afraid. And the angel said to them, Fear not: for behold, I bring you good tidings of great joy, which shall be to all people. For unto you is born this day in the city of David a Saviour, which is Christ the Lord.

And this shall be a sign unto you; Ye shall find the babe wrapped in swaddling clothes, lying in a manger. And suddenly there was with the angel a multitude of the heavenly host praising God, and saying,

Glory to God in the highest, and on earth peace, good will toward men.

And it came to pass, as the angels were gone away from them into heaven, the shepherds said one to another, Let us now go even unto Bethlehem, and see this thing which is come to pass, which the Lord hath made known unto us. And they came with haste, and found Mary, and Joseph, and the babe lying in a manger. And when they had seen it, they made known abroad the saying which was told them

concerning this child. And all they that heard it wondered at those things which were told them by the shepherds.

Now when Jesus was born in Bethlehem of Judæa in the days of Herod the king, behold, there came wise men from the east to Jerusalem, saying, Where is he that is born King of the Jews? for we have seen his star in the east, and are come to worship him.

When Herod the king had heard these things, he was troubled, and all Jerusalem with him. And when he had gathered all the chief priests and scribes of the people together, he demanded of them where Christ should be born. And they said unto him, In Bethlehem of Judæa: for thus it is written by the prophet, And thou Bethlehem, in the land of Juda, art not the least among the princes of Juda: for out of thee shall come a Governor, that shall rule my people Israel.

Then Herod, when he had privily called the wise men, inquired of them diligently what time the star appeared. And he sent them to Bethlehem, and said, Go and search diligently for the young child; and when ye have found him, bring me word again, that I may come and worship him also. When they had heard the king, they departed; and lo, the star, which they saw in the east, went before them, till it came and stood over where the young child was. When they saw the star, they rejoiced with exceeding great joy.

And when they were come into the house, they saw the young child with Mary his mother, and fell down, and worshipped him: and when they had opened their treasures, they presented unto him gifts; gold, frankincense, and myrrh.

And being warned of God in a dream that they should not return to Herod, they departed into their own country another way.

And when they were departed, behold, the angel of the Lord appeareth to Joseph in a dream, saying, Arise, and take the young child and his mother, and flee into Egypt, and be thou there until I bring thee word: for Herod will seek the young child to destroy him.

When he arose, he took the young child and his mother by night, and departed into Egypt: And was there until the death of Herod: that it might be fulfilled which was spoken of the Lord by the prophet saying, Out of Egypt have I called my son.

Away in a Manger

Martin Luther

Away in a manger,
no crib for his bed,
the little Lord Jesus
lay down his sweet head.
The stars in the sky
looked down where he lay,
the little Lord Jesus,
asleep on the hay.

The cattle are lowing,
the poor baby wakes,
but little Lord Jesus,
no crying he makes;
I love thee, Lord Jesus,
look down from the sky,
and stay by my cradle
till morning is nigh.

Be near me, Lord Jesus,
I ask thee to stay
close by me forever
and love me, I pray:
Bless all the dear children
in thy tender care,
and take us to heaven
to live with thee there.

14

so up to the housetop the coursers they flew
with a sleigh full of toys and Saint Nicholas too.

And then in a twinkling I heard on the roof
the prancing and pawing of each little hoof.
As I drew in my head and was turning around,
down the chimney Saint Nicholas came with a bound.

He was dressed all in fur from his head to his foot,
and his clothes were all tarnished with ashes and soot.
A bundle of toys he had flung on his back,
and he looked like a peddler just opening his pack.

His eyes—how they twinkled! His dimples—how merry!
His cheeks were like roses, his nose like a cherry!
His droll little mouth was drawn up like a bow,
and the beard on his chin was as white as the snow.

The stump of a pipe he held tight in his teeth,
and the smoke it encircled his head like a wreath.
He had a broad face and a little round belly
that shook when he laughed like a bowl full of jelly.

He was chubby and plump, a right jolly old elf,
and I laughed when I saw him in spite of myself.
A wink of his eye and a twist of his head
soon gave me to know I had nothing to dread.

He spoke not a word, but went straight to his work,
and filled all the stockings; then turned with a jerk;
and laying a finger aside of his nose
and giving a nod, up the chimney he rose;

He sprang to his sleigh, to his team gave a whistle,
and away they all flew like the down of a thistle.
But I heard him exclaim ere he drove out of sight,
"Happy Christmas to all and to all a good night!"

Joy to the World
Isaac Watts

Joy to the world! The Lord is come:
Let earth receive her king.
Let ev'ry heart prepare him room
and heav'n and nature sing,
and heav'n and nature sing,
and heaven and heaven and nature sing.

Joy to the earth! The savior reigns:
Let men their songs employ;
while fields and floods, rocks, hills and plains,
repeat the sounding joy,
repeat the sounding joy,
repeat, repeat the sounding joy.

He rules the world with truth and grace,
And makes the nations prove
The glories of his righteousness,
And wonders of his love,
And wonders of his love,
And wonders, wonders of his love.

15

The Night before Christmas

Clement C. Moore

'Twas the night before Christmas, when all through the house
not a creature was stirring, not even a mouse.
The stockings were hung by the chimney with care
in hopes that Saint Nicholas soon would be there.

The children were nestled all snug in their beds
while visions of sugarplums danced in their heads.
And Mama in her kerchief and I in my cap
had just settled down for a long winter's nap.

When out on the lawn there arose such a clatter,
I sprang from my bed to see what was the matter.
Away to the window I flew like a flash,
tore open the shutters and threw up the sash.

The moon on the breast of the new-fallen snow
gave a luster of midday to objects below.
When what to my wondering eyes should appear,
but a miniature sleigh and eight tiny reindeer,

With a little old driver so lively and quick,
I knew in a moment it must be Saint Nick.
More rapid than eagles, his coursers they came
and he whistled and shouted and called them by name,

"Now, Dasher! Now, Dancer! Now, Prancer and Vixen!
On, Comet! On, Cupid! On, Donder and Blitzen!
To the top of the porch, to the top of the wall,
now dash away! Dash away! Dash away, all!"

As dry leaves that before the wild hurricane fly,
when they meet with an obstacle, mount to the sky,

Yes, Virginia, There Is a Santa Claus

from *The New York Sun*, September 21, 1897

We take pleasure in answering at once and thus prominently the communication below, expressing at the same time our great gratification that its faithful author is numbered among the friends of *The Sun*:

Dear Editor:

I am eight years old.

Some of my little friends say there is no Santa Claus.

Papa says, "If you see it in *The Sun*, it's so."

Please tell me the truth, is there a Santa Claus?

—Virginia O'Hanlon,
115 West 95th Street

Virginia, your little friends are wrong. They have been affected by the skepticism of a skeptical age. They do not believe except they see. They think that nothing can be which is not comprehensible by their little minds. All minds, Virginia, whether they be men's or children's, are little. In this great universe of ours, man is a mere insect, an ant, in his intellect, as compared with the boundless world about him, as measured by the intelligence capable of grasping the whole of truth and knowledge.

Yes, Virginia, there is a Santa Claus. He exists as certainly as love and generosity and devotion exist; and you know that they abound and give to your life its highest beauty and joy. Alas! how dreary would be the world if there were no Santa Claus! It

would be as dreary as if there were no Virginias. There would be no childlike faith then, no poetry, no romance to make tolerable this existence. We should have no enjoyment, except in sense and sight. The eternal light with which childhood fills the world would be extinguished.

Not believe in Santa Claus! You might as well not believe in fairies! You might get your papa to hire men to watch in all the chimneys on Christmas Eve to catch Santa Claus, but even if they did not see Santa Claus coming down, what would that prove? Nobody sees Santa Claus, but that is no sign that there is no Santa Claus. The most real things in the world are those that neither children nor men can see. Did you ever see fairies dancing on the lawn? Of course not, but that's no proof that they are not there. Nobody can conceive or imagine all the wonders there are unseen and unseeable in the world.

You tear apart the baby's rattle and see what makes the noise inside; but there is a veil covering the unseen world which not the strongest man, nor even the united strength of the strongest men that ever lived, could tear apart. Only faith, fancy, poetry, love, romance, can push aside that curtain and view and picture the supernal beauty and glory beyond. Is it all real? Yes, Virginia, in all this world there is nothing else real and abiding.

No Santa Claus! Thank God he lives, and he lives forever. A thousand years from now, Virginia, nay, ten times ten thousand years from now, he will continue to make glad the heart of childhood.

—Francis P. Church

We Wish You a Merry Christmas

Traditional

We wish you a merry Christmas,
we wish you a merry Christmas,
we wish you a merry Christmas,
and a happy New Year.

Good tidings we bring for you and your kin.
We wish you a merry Christmas, and a happy New Year.

Oh, bring us some figgy pudding,
oh, bring us some figgy pudding,
oh, bring us some figgy pudding,
now bring some right here.

Good tidings we bring for you and your kin.
We wish you a merry Christmas, and a happy New Year.

We won't go until we get some,
we won't go until we get some,
we won't go until we get some,
so bring some right here.

Good tidings we bring for you and your kin.
We wish you a merry Christmas, and a happy New Year.

O Christmas Tree

(O Tannenbaum)
Traditional

O Christmas tree, O Christmas tree,
with faithful leaves unchanging;
O Christmas tree, O Christmas tree
with faithful leaves unchanging;
not only green in summer's heat,
but also winter's snow and sleet;
O Christmas tree, O Christmas tree
with faithful leaves unchanging.

O Christmas tree, O Christmas tree,
of all the trees most lovely;
O Christmas tree, O Christmas tree,
of all the trees most lovely;
each year you bring to me delight,
gleaming in the Christmas night;
O Christmas tree, O Christmas tree,
of all the trees most lovely.

O Christmas tree, O Christmas tree,
your leaves will teach me also;
O Christmas tree, O Christmas tree,
your leaves will teach me also;
That love and hope and faithfulness
are precious things I can possess;
O Christmas tree, O Christmas tree,
your leaves will teach me also.

The Fir Tree

Hans Christian Andersen

Out in the forest stood a pretty little fir tree. It grew in a lovely spot with plenty of sunlight and air, and all around it grew many larger trees. But the little fir tree wished very much to become greater. It did not care for the warm sun and fresh air; it took no notice of the peasant children who came out to look for the berries. The children would sit down by the little fir tree and say, "How pretty and small that one is!" The tree did not like to hear that at all.

"Oh, if I were only as great a tree as the others!" sighed the little fir.

When it was winter and the snow lay all around, a hare would often come jumping along and spring right over the little fir. This made the tree so angry.

"Oh! To grow! To grow and become old—that's the only fine thing in the world," said the tree longingly.

When Christmastime approached, many young trees were cut down—some which were neither so old nor so large as this fir tree. These young trees, which were always the most beautiful, were carefully put upon wagons, and horses dragged them out of the woods.

"Where are all those trees going?" asked the fir tree.

"We know where they go," chirped the sparrows. "We have looked through the windows of the houses. Those trees are planted in the middle of warm rooms and are adorned with beautiful things."

"And then?" asked the fir tree. "What happens then?"

"Why, we haven't seen anything more," answered the sparrows.

"If only it were Christmas now!" cried the fir tree. "Now I am grown-up, like the trees who were taken away. If only I were in the warm room amid all the splendor!"

"Rejoice in your fresh youth here in the woodland," said the air and sunshine.

But the fir tree did not rejoice, and at Christmastime it was cut down before any of the others. An ax cut deep into its marrow, and it fell to the ground with a sigh.

As the tree was unloaded in a yard, it heard a man say, "We want this tree!"

Two servants came and carried the fir tree into a beautiful room and put it into a tub filled with sand. Then the fir tree was decorated with little nets of colored paper, golden apples, walnuts, dolls, and more than a hundred little candles, and high on the summit of the tree was fixed a tinsel star. The little fir tree looked splendid.

At last the candles were lighted, the doors were thrown open, and the children hurried in, shouting till the room rang. They ran forward to strip the tree of presents, rushing on it so that every branch cracked and groaned. If it had not been fastened by the top to the ceiling, the fir tree would have fallen down.

"A story! A story!" shouted the children as they drew a little fat man toward the tree. And the fat man told a story about Klumpey-Dumpey, who fell downstairs, was honored, and finally married a princess. The fir tree stood quite silent and thoughtful; never had the birds in the woods told such a story as that.

And the fir tree looked forward with pleasure to being adorned again with candles and toys, gold and fruit on the next evening. "Tomorrow," it sighed, "I will rejoice in all my splendor. Tomorrow I shall hear the story of Klumpey-Dumpey again."

In the morning, the servants came in. Now my splendor will begin afresh, thought the tree. But they dragged the tree into a dark corner of the attic.

What's the meaning of this? the tree wondered. What am I to do here?

Days and nights went by, and nobody came up to see it. The tree had been forgotten. The tree supposed it was being sheltered till spring when it could be planted again. The attic was dark and the tree was terribly lonely.

"Squeak!" said a little mouse as he crept forward. Then another one came closer. "Where do you come from?" asked the mice. "Have you been in the storeroom where the cheeses lie on the shelves and the hams hang from the ceiling?"

"No," said the tree, "but I can tell you about the woods, where the sun shines and the birds sing." And the tree told them all about its youth.

The mice listened and said, "How happy you must have been!"

"Happy?" said the fir tree. "Yes, those were really quite merry days." Then it told them all about Christmas Eve, when it had been hung with gifts and candles.

"What stories you can tell!" said the little mice.

The next night they came with four other little mice to hear the tree. The more the tree told them, the more it remembered.

Then the fir tree told the story of Klumpey-Dumpey. It could remember every single word, and the little mice were ready to leap to the top of the tree with pleasure. The next night more mice and even two rats appeared.

"Do you know only one story?" asked the rats. "Don't you know stories about bacon and tallow candles—a storeroom story?"

"No," replied the tree.

"Then we'd rather not hear," said the rats. They and the mice went back home.

One morning, people came into the attic and the tree was dragged outside.

"Now I shall live!" said the tree joyfully. But its limbs were all withered and yellow, and the tree was cast into the corner among the weeds. Several children were playing in the courtyard. One ran up and tore off the star, then trod on the branches.

The tree wished it had remained in the dark attic. It thought of its fresh youth in the woods, of the merry Christmas Eve, and of the little mice that had listened so eagerly to its stories.

"Past!" said the old tree. "If I had only rejoiced when I could have done so!"

A servant came and chopped the tree into pieces. And then the fir tree was burned. As it blazed brightly, it sighed deeply, crackling and popping with each sigh.

The children played in the garden, and the youngest had the golden star which the tree had worn on its happiest evening. Now that was past, and the tree's life was past, and this story is past too. Past! Past! And that's the way it is with all stories.

We Three Kings

J.H. Hopkins, Jr.

We three kings of orient are, bearing gifts we traverse afar,
field and fountain, moor and mountain, following yonder star.

O star of wonder, star of night! Star of royal beauty bright;
westward leading, still proceeding, guide us to thy perfect light.

Born a king on Bethlehem plain, gold I bring to crown him again,
king forever ceasing never, over us all to reign.

O star of wonder, star of night! Star of royal beauty bright;
westward leading, still proceeding, guide us to thy perfect light.

Frankincense to offer have I, incense owns a deity nigh:
Prayer and praising, all men raising; worship him, God on high.

O star of wonder, star of night! Star of royal beauty bright;
westward leading, still proceeding, guide us to thy perfect light.

Myrrh is mine; its bitter perfume breathes a life of gathering gloom;
Sorrowing, sighing, bleeding, dying, sealed in the stone cold tomb.

O star of wonder, star of night! Star of royal beauty bright;
westward leading, still proceeding, guide us to thy perfect light.

The First Noel

Traditional

The first noel, the angel did say,
was to certain poor shepherds in fields as they lay;
in fields where they lay keeping their sheep,
on a cold winter's night that was so deep.

Noel, noel, noel, noel! Born is the king of Israel!

They looked up and saw a star
shining in the east beyond them far.
And to the earth it gave great light,
and so it continued both day and night.

Noel, noel, noel, noel! Born is the king of Israel!

And by the light of that same star,
three wise men came from country far;
to seek for a king was their intent,
and to follow the star wherever it went.

Noel, noel, noel, noel! Born is the king of Israel!

This star drew nigh to the northwest,
over Bethlehem it took its rest,
and there it did both stop and stay,
right over the place where Jesus lay.

Noel, noel, noel, noel! Born is the king of Israel!

Then entered in those wise men three,
full reverently upon the knee,
and offered there, in his presence,
their gold, and myrrh, and frankincense.

Noel, noel, noel, noel! Born is the king of Israel!

The Nutcracker

Based on *The Nutcracker and the Mouse King* by E.T.A. Hoffman
and *The Nutcracker Ballet* by Peter Ilyich Tschaikovsky

Twelve-year-old Clara Stahlbaum knelt by the parlor door, peeking through the keyhole into the drawing room. Her brother, Fritz, crouched next to her, and behind him stood eight other children.

"What do you see?" asked Fritz.

"Nothing yet," she replied. "The grown-ups are just dancing and talking."

A moment later the door swung open and the parlor was flooded with light. Dr. Stahlbaum stood there beaming.

"Merry Christmas, children!" he said.

They raced past him into the drawing room, with Fritz leading the way and Clara following close behind. Before them stood a Christmas tree at least ten feet tall.

Beneath the tree were sugarplums, bonbons, toy soldiers, miniature swords and cannons, ceramic dolls, silk dresses, wooden horses, picture books, and dozens of other gifts. The children scurried about, discovering treasure after treasure.

Then the front door burst open, and out of the winter night stepped a man dressed in black. A tall hat covered his head, and he held a cape over his face. The man strode up to the group, the click of his boots echoing off the marble floor. Then he stopped and slowly drew aside the cape. Beneath it was the smiling face of Godpapa Drosselmeier, known throughout the village as a master woodcarver.

"Oh, Godpapa," cried Clara, "you scared us!" Clara's godfather gave her a big hug.

"My dear," he said, "I've brought you and the other children a surprise." He drew the sides of his cape together in a great circle, and when he opened them, three wooden figures stood on the floor in front of him: a prince, a princess, and a wicked-looking mouse wearing a crown. The figures began to move.

The mouse challenged the prince, they drew their swords, and a fight began. The

children shouted encouragement. Finally, the prince defeated the mouse king, and then he kneeled, kissing the princess softly on her outstretched hand. It seemed for a moment that Clara could feel the kiss on her own hand.

When the wooden figures stopped moving, the guests clapped and cheered. Godpapa Drosselmeier took a bow, then turned to Clara. "And now," he said, "I have one more surprise. It's a special gift for a very special girl."

Godpapa drew his cape aside, and there stood another wooden figure wearing a handsome military uniform. Its face, though, was not handsome. Brightly painted, it had enormous eyes and a wide, gaping mouth. And something about the face filled Clara with tenderness. She picked up the figure and cradled it in her arms.

"What is it?" asked one of the children looking on.

"It's a nutcracker," replied Clara's godfather. Then he took a walnut from his pocket and placed it in the little man's mouth. The mouth closed and broke the nut.

"Let me do that!" said Fritz. He grabbed the nutcracker and tried to pull it away from his sister. There was a loud crack, and the wooden figure's head broke off.

"He's ruined!" Clara cried, holding her precious gift close and weeping bitterly.

"Now, now, my dear," said Godpapa Drosselmeier, taking the nutcracker. He put the wooden figure back together, and the nutcracker was as good as new.

Several hours later, after the family had gone to bed, Clara lay in her room, thinking about the nutcracker. She slipped out of her bed and down the stairs.

The drawing room was dark, but Clara had no trouble picking out the brightly painted face of the nutcracker beneath the Christmas tree. She went over to her new friend, lay down beside him, and fell into a deep sleep.

Suddenly, there was a noise in the room. Clara awoke and peered into the darkness. Slinking toward her was a mouse as big as a man. The mouse was joined by ten others just like it. They circled around her, drawing closer and closer. When they were near enough to touch, the clock chimed the first stroke of midnight.

Next to her, the nutcracker moved. Yawning and stretching, he rose to his feet. Then, as the clock kept striking, he began to grow. By the time the twelfth chime died, he was Nutcracker, a real-life soldier standing six feet tall.

Clara watched as Nutcracker put one arm around her and, with the other, drew

his sword. The mice backed away. There was a puff of smoke and out stepped another mouse. Bigger and uglier than the others, he was the evil Mouse King. Encouraged by the arrival of their leader, the other mice edged forward once again.

A bugle sounded from the direction of the Christmas tree. Clara watched in astonishment as the toy soldiers grew to full size. Under Nutcracker's orders, they fired their cannon and advanced on the mice. A tremendous struggle followed. First one side, then the other appeared to be winning. The room filled with the sounds of battle. Nutcracker and the Mouse King crossed swords. The two leaders circled, thrusting and parrying, as Clara shouted encouragement from the side.

Then it happened. The Mouse King lunged and Nutcracker went down. But Nutcracker struggled to his feet, his face contorted in pain, and challenged the Mouse King once again. The ugly gray creature closed in to finish him off.

Clara saw the flash of Nutcracker's sword and the sudden halt of his opponent. The Mouse King lay dead on the floor, and Nutcracker had fallen motionless beside him. The mice took the body of their leader and carried it off, their steps slow.

Clara, meanwhile, rushed to the fallen Nutcracker and knelt beside him. She took his hand and smoothed his brow, searching for signs of life. She saw none.

In the silence, there were footsteps. Clara looked up and saw her godfather standing over her. She threw herself into his arms.

"Oh, Godpapa," she cried, "what can I do?"

Her godfather held her close and murmured, "Now, now, my dear, Godpapa will fix your dream." He touched the warrior's shoulder. Nutcracker's eyes popped open.

Clara gasped, then watched in awe as his face began to change. The bright colors melted together, and the gaping mouth and eyes took on a pleasing shape. Seconds later, Clara was looking at a dashing prince.

"Thank you, Godpapa," she said, hugging the old man tight. "Thank you for saving him." Then the prince rose to his feet. Kneeling, he kissed Clara's hand.

Suddenly, Clara was back in the drawing room, alone on the floor cradling a small wooden nutcracker. She went to the front door and peered out into the night.

Snow was falling in the streets of the village, but Clara didn't see it. She was looking beyond to a land where toys spring to life and goodness always wins.

Up on the Housetop

Benjamin R. Hanby

Up on the housetop reindeer pause,
out jumps good old Santa Claus.
Down through the chimney with lots of toys,
all for the little ones' Christmas joys.

Ho, ho, ho! Who wouldn't go!
Ho, ho, ho! Who wouldn't go!
Up on the housetop, click, click, click,
down through the chimney with good Saint Nick.

First comes the stocking of little Nell;
oh, dear Santa fill it well.
Give her a dolly that laughs and cries,
one that will open and shut her eyes.

Ho, ho, ho! Who wouldn't go!
Ho, ho, ho! Who wouldn't go!
Up on the housetop, click, click, click,
down through the chimney with good Saint Nick.

Next comes the stocking of little Will,
oh, just see what a glorious fill.
Here is a hammer and lots of tacks,
also a ball and whip that cracks.

Ho, ho, ho! Who wouldn't go!
Ho, ho, ho! Who wouldn't go!
Up on the housetop, click, click, click,
down through the chimney with good Saint Nick.

The Twelve Days of Christmas
Traditional

On the first day of Christmas, my true love sent to me a partridge in a pear tree.

On the second day of Christmas, my true love sent to me two turtle doves and a partridge in a pear tree.

On the third day of Christmas, my true love sent to me three French hens, two turtle doves, and a partridge in a pear tree.

On the fourth day of Christmas, my true love sent to me four calling birds, three French hens, two turtle doves, and a partridge in a pear tree.

On the fifth day of Christmas, my true love sent to me five golden rings, four calling birds, three French hens, two turtle doves, and a partridge in a pear tree.

On the sixth day of Christmas, my true love sent to me six geese a-laying, five golden rings, four calling birds, three French hens, two turtle doves, and a partridge in a pear tree.

On the seventh day of Christmas, my true love sent to me seven swans a-swimming, six geese a-laying, five golden rings, four calling birds, three French hens, two turtle doves, and a partridge in a pear tree.

On the eighth day of Christmas, my true love sent to me eight maids a-milking, seven swans a-swimming, six geese a-laying, five golden rings, four calling birds, three French hens, two turtle doves, and a partridge in a pear tree.

On the ninth day of Christmas, my true love sent to me nine ladies dancing, eight maids a-milking, seven swans a-swimming, six geese a-laying, five golden rings, four calling birds, three French hens, two turtle doves, and a partridge in a pear tree.

On the tenth day of Christmas, my true love sent to me ten lords a-leaping, nine ladies dancing, eight maids a-milking, seven swans a-swimming, six geese a-laying, five golden rings, four calling birds, three French hens, two turtle doves, and a partridge in a pear tree.

On the eleventh day of Christmas, my true love sent to me eleven pipers piping, ten lords a-leaping, nine ladies dancing, eight maids a-milking, seven swans a-swimming, six geese a-laying, five golden rings, four calling birds, three French hens, two turtle doves, and a partridge in a pear tree.

On the twelfth day of Christmas, my true love sent to me twelve drummers drumming, eleven pipers piping, ten lords a-leaping, nine ladies dancing, eight maids a-milking, seven swans a-swimming, six geese a-laying, five golden rings, four calling birds, three French hens, two turtle doves, and a partridge in a pear tree.